FAMOUS 5 ON THE CASE

LOOK OUT FOR THE WHOLE SERIES!

Case Files 1 & 2: The Case of the Fudgie Fry Pirates & The Case of the Plant that Could Eat Your House

Case Files 3 & 4: The Case of the Impolite Snarly Thing & The Case of the Sticks and Their Tricks

Case Files 5 & 6: The Case of the Plot to Pull the Plug & The Case of the Thief Who Drinks from the Toilet

Case Files 7 & 8: The Case of the Hot-Air Ba-Boom! & The Case of the Stinky Smell

Case Files 9 & 10: The Case of the Defective Detective & The Case of Allie's Really Very Bad Singing

Case Files 11 & 12: The Case of the Medieval Meathead & The Case of the Messy Mucked Up Masterpiece

Case Files 13 & 14: The Case of the Guy Who Makes You Act Like a Chicken & The Case of the Felon with Frosty Fingers

Case Files 15 & 16: The Case of the Bogus Banknotes & The Case of Eight Arms and No Fingerprints

Case Files 17 & 18: The Case of the Flowers That Make Your Body All Wobbly & The Case of the Guy Who Looks Pretty Good for a 2000 Year-Old

Case Files 19 & 20: The Case of the Gobbling Goop & The Case of the Surfer Dude Who's Truly Rude

Case Files 21 & 22: The Case of the Cactus, the Coot, and the Cowboy Boot & The Case of the Seal Who Gets All Up In Your Face

Case Files 23 & 24: The Case of the Snow, the Glow, and the Oh, No! & The Case of the Fish That Flew the Coop

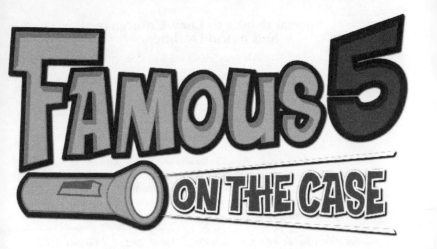

FAMOUS 5 ON THE CASE

THE CASE OF THE FELON WITH FROSTY FINGERS

Hodder Children's Books

A division of Hachette Children's Books

Special thanks to Lucy Courtenay and Artful Doodlers

First published in Great Britain in 2008 by Hodder Children's Books

1

A Catalogue record for this book is available from the British Library

ISBN 978 0 340 97084 3

Typeset in Weiss by Avon DataSet Ltd,
Bidford on Avon, Warwickshire

Printed and bound in Great Britain by
Bookmarque Ltd, Croydon, Surrey

The paper and board used in this paperback by Hodder Children's Books are natural recyclable products made from wood grown in sustainable forests. The manufacturing processes conform to the environmental regulations of the country of origin.

Hodder Children's Books
a division of Hachette Children's Books
338 Euston Road, London NW1 3BH
An Hachette Livre UK Company
www.hachettelivre.co.uk

Chapter One

The moon hung low in the sky and the stars were still twinkling when an alarm clock shattered the early morning stillness.

RRRRIIIIIINNNNGGGG!

Three bleary-eyed, sleepy teenagers staggered into the kitchen. Allie leaned up against the wall and tried to go back to sleep. Dylan did better, collapsing onto a chair and nodding off, his glasses halfway down his nose. Max missed his own chair completely, and sank to the floor.

"Good morning!" said Jo brightly, stroking her dog Timmy beside the kitchen sink. "It's five a.m. Hidey-ho!"

Max opened one eye and peered out from under his even-more-bedhead-than-usual fringe. "Wow," he yawned. "I don't like the look of five a.m."

"Is this some kind of impromptu fire drill?" Dylan complained. "Or are you just plain evil?"

"Mum's away and Cleopatra must be milked," Jo said in a bossy sort of way. "That's done at five a.m. Haven't you learned anything about the country?"

"I just learned I don't like five a.m," Max growled.

Jo led the way out of the house and across the dark farmyard. The others followed, still half-asleep. She unlatched the door and they all stepped inside the barn. Several photos of Cleopatra hung on the wall. There was a snap of the prize cow as a calf, and one of her wearing a blue ribbon. There was even one of Cleopatra's wedding day with the local bull.

"Lovely veil," Allie said, peering at the wedding shot. "Vintage. And yet it's on a cow."

"Not just a cow," Jo said, sounding offended. "More like a member of the family. Smellier than Dylan, but quieter." She glanced around. "So," she said, "the bucket and milking stool are kept there . . ."

Obediently, Dylan fetched the bucket and milk stool.

"The clean straw is kept over there," Jo said, pointing across the stall.

Max lay down gratefully on the straw and fell asleep at once.

"The milking bridle is kept over . . . here," Jo continued.

Timmy fetched the bridle.

"One question," Allie said, peering inside Cleopatra's stall. "Where is the cow kept?"

Jo rushed over to look into the stall.

It was empty.

Chapter Two

"Maybe aliens are studying Cleopatra and they'll return her when they're done," Max suggested from his cosy spot on the straw, as Jo rushed frantically around the barn looking for the cow. "Then she could write a book about it."

"I think we can count on that!" Dylan agreed, in the bright voice he used whenever Max launched into one of his alien theories. "Meanwhile, the facts are Cleopatra disappeared sometime early this morning."

"Early, *early* this morning," Allie said between yawns. She was having trouble staying on her feet, even with Timmy pushing her upright with his nose.

Jo pounced on Cleopatra's stall rope. "And she didn't just wander off," she said, shaking the rope at the others. "The rope has been cut!"

"Severed by an alien laser beam . . ." Max offered in a sing-song told-you-so voice.

Jo noticed a piece of red material hanging on a gate nail. "Must be from the thief's clothing," she said, snatching it up. "Some kind of fibre – red fibre."

"A lumberjack!" Max said. "In long underwear!"

Dylan stared at his cousin. "You're not really awake, are you?" he said.

"Not even close," Max mumbled, rolling over in the straw and starting to snore.

Timmy sniffed at something buried in the straw. He picked up an old ice-lolly stick and held it out to Allie.

"Somebody was eating an ice lolly," said Allie, taking the stick and examining it.

Max got up. "Ice lolly? I'm awake." He took the stick from Allie and sniffed it expertly. "Lime sorbet," he decided. "No – lemon."

They could see that the stick had a picture of a rugby ball on it.

"Never seen an ice-lolly stick like that before," Dylan said with a frown.

"Well, we've got plenty of clues to work with," Jo said. "I think we know what our next move is."

"Yes," Max agreed, with a massive yawn. "Sleep." He collapsed backwards into a soft-looking pile of hay, leaping up again immediately. "Oww!" he wailed, rubbing his bottom. "Pitchfork! I'm awake . . ."

* * *

Later on, Jo sat at the desk in her mother's study in front of a microscope. She took a pair of tweezers and picked up the red fibre. Then, as she went to place it carefully on the microscope slide, Constable Stubblefield – the officer in charge at Falcongate Police Station – put her head around the door.

"Kirrin offspring!" said Constable Stubblefield in a loud and cheerful voice. "Hello!"

Startled, Jo dropped both the tweezers and the slide.

"Constable Stubblefield," Max said as Jo bent down with a sigh to pick everything up, "Aunt George's cow's been stolen."

"Her rope was cut, we found some red fibre and an ice-lolly stick," Dylan put in.

For once, it really looked as if Constable Stubblefield was concentrating on what the cousins were saying. "Hold on . . ." she said. "I've got it . . ."

Then again, maybe not. Constable Stubblefield had picked up a magazine and was now swatting something on the table. "Yes – got you, fly!" she said triumphantly. She put down the magazine.

"Interesting," she said, coming back to the question of Cleopatra's disappearance. "A lot of cows in the area have gone missing lately."

"Don't you think you should investigate?" Dylan suggested.

"Of course I'll investigate!" Constable Stubblefield declared. "Soon as I get back from my Romance Novel Convention," she added, "it's on top of my in-tray."

She beckoned to someone who was standing just behind her. Into the room came an adorable six-year-old girl wearing pigtails and noisily chewing on bubble gum. Glancing around, she waved shyly at everyone.

"Meanwhile, as we arranged, here's my niece, Victoria," Constable Stubblefield said, placing rather a heavy hand on the little girl's shoulder.

Allie knelt down. "Hi, Victoria!" she said cheerfully.

The others looked confused.

"I promised I'd babysit," Allie explained. She turned back to the little girl. "How big a bubble can you blow, Victoria?"

Victoria blew an enormous bubble, which

popped in Allie's face and covered her in pink goo.

"Ewww," Allie said weakly, wiping the gum from her face. "Bigger than I thought."

"I'm off," said Constable Stubblefield, rubbing her hands. "Fantastico, the muscly guy from the book covers, is giving a seminar on Smouldering Glances." The police officer demonstrated a few smouldering glances of her own, then looked a bit swoony.

"Ahhh, Fantastico . . . !" she murmured, "it's a good day to be Stubblefield."

As the police officer danced out of the room and off to her squad car, Allie took Victoria over to a big, elaborate doll's house that stood in the corner of the study. "Look at all the dolls, Victoria!" she said enthusiastically. "I love dolls because you use your imagination when you play with them." She pointed at each doll in turn. "This is Tyler and Skye. They were adopted by an international superstar couple. They're orphans by day and superheroes by night."

"That's silly," said Victoria in a clear, high voice.

"Oh," said Allie, a little deflated. "I thought it

was pretty good. Anyway, have fun. Make things up. Be creative." And she left the little girl to it.

Unwisely, as it turned out.

Chapter Three

Jo beckoned Allie over to the microscope as Victoria started playing with the dolls. "Allie, what do you make of this red fibre?" she asked.

"Synthetic blend . . ." Allie murmured, looking through the lens. "Cheap . . . Scratchy. Doesn't breathe."

The others glanced at each other. What was their ditzy cousin talking about?

"I know my fabrics," Allie explained.

Dylan was at his laptop. The ice-lolly stick was in his hand. "I can't find an ice-lolly company that has rugby balls on its sticks," he sighed, pushing away from the screen. "Maybe we should talk to an ice-lolly expert."

Max put up his hand. "Yes, how can I help you?"

Jo rolled her eyes. "Somebody who *makes* them, not *eats* them," she said. "Like Father Goose. His factory's right near here and it's open to the public."

SMASH!

Aghast, Allie rushed over to the doll's house. It had been crushed to splinters. Victoria sat in the wreckage.

"You told me to use my imagination," Victoria said, smiling happily. "I imagined the house was full of mean, rich people. I tore it down to make a hospital for poor people."

Max looked impressed. "That's better than the superhero thing," he told Allie.

Victoria daintily took the dolls out of the wreckage. "Now I imagine the dolls are angels who can fly!" she announced. "Fly angels, fly!"

Allie ducked as the little girl started flinging dolls at the Kirrins. Everyone leaped out of the way, doing their best to stop the dolls from knocking things off the shelves. Dylan caught a falling vase. Jo grabbed two or three snow globes. Timmy caught a framed picture of himself in his mouth.

Max saved a delicate china figurine, but before he could feel too pleased with himself a large book fell down on his head.

"Owww," he wailed, rubbing his head. "Now that's a heavy read." Another book caught him on the ear. "Oww!"

Later that day, the cousins and their small friend stood at the entrance to a large red-brick Victorian building on a hillside above Falcongate. Beside the factory was a large barn, from which came the sound of mooing. It was Father Goose's ice-cream factory.

Inside, it was bitterly cold. Huge stainless-steel ice-cream machines churned away as the Five breathed out mistily, wishing they had brought their jumpers. Workers were bustling in and out of the Tasting Room, which was decorated in nursery-rhyme style, with swings and see-saws and even a Jack and Jill well. Two workers dressed as Gingerbread Men were offering free samples.

Max didn't know where to look. "Wow," he said in a daze, "free ice cream. This is the greatest place in the entire world. I'm going to live here."

Victoria raced over to a see-saw, clutching her ice cream. She sat down on one end of the see-saw, making the other end fly up and crash her back down. Her ice cream sailed into the air and splattered all over Allie's top. "Oops, sorry," she giggled.

"That's OK," Allie said a little stiffly. "It only cost me four months' allowance."

"That's funny, then!" Victoria laughed. She pointed across the room in excitement. "Costumes! Yay!"

She scampered over to a large old trunk in the corner of the room, which was full of dressing-up clothes. She started pulling out nursery-rhyme outfits.

"Max, you be Little Bo Peep!" she squealed, thrusting a frilly dress at Max.

The others burst out laughing as Max pulled on the costume quite seriously. "I happen to be comfortable enough with my masculinity to be Little Bo Peep," Max told them, tying his bonnet under his chin with a floppy bow. He raised his hands and started wailing: "Oh, I have lost my sheep and don't know where to find them!"

The others doubled over as Max rushed back and forth, skipping a little. "Oh my!" he trilled in a falsetto voice. "Oooff . . ."

He had run smack into a round-bellied, ruddy-faced man in a flamboyant Edwardian outfit: Father Goose himself.

"You strike me as more of a Peter Peter Pumpkin-Eater than a Bo Peep," said Father Goose as a blushing Max untangled his ribbons from where they'd got wrapped round the factory owner's watch chain. "But if you love ice cream, you're all right in my book."

Chapter Four

"Father Goose, could we ask you a couple of questions?" Jo asked.

"That's one question already!" Father Goose pointed out. "Ha, ha, ha, ha, ha, ha, ha, ha!" He paused to take a deep breath. "Ah-ha, ha, ha, ha, ha, ha, ha!" he hooted. "Ho-ho-ho!"

The kids glanced at each other. Father Goose was – a bit odd.

"Wah-ha, ha, ha, ha!" guffawed the unusual factory owner.

"He's weird," said Victoria in a loud voice.

"Victoria, look!" said Allie brightly, keen to avoid any more embarrassment. "Free ice cream! And chocolate dipping syrup!"

She grabbed the six-year-old's hand and showed her to an ice cream buffet where lots of different ice cream flavours and trimmings waited for customers.

"Can I dip *anything*?!" Victoria gasped.

"Sure!" said Allie, returning to the others. "Get creative!"

Jo was still asking Father Goose questions. "My mum's cow was stolen," she said. "We were wondering if any of yours were, too?"

"No, thank heaven," said Father Goose. "They're all in the barn, snug as Mary's little lamb."

"We have this stick," Dylan said, showing Father Goose the ice-lolly stick.

"Really?" said Father Goose encouragingly. He patted Dylan on the shoulder. "Good for you! I'm sure you're quite proud of it!"

"We were wondering if you recognized the rugby ball logo," Dylan pressed on.

Father Goose looked at the stick. His face fell. "Unfortunately I do," he said. "Those rugby sticks are part of an upcoming promotion by Wally Caldwell."

"The rugby player?!" Max gasped. He turned to

the others. "He badly injured his knee last season and had to retire," he explained. "He was pretty angry about it."

"He's angry about everything," said Father Goose sadly. "He's moved to our area to make ice cream. In my opinion, he can sit on Miss Muffet's Tuffet."

Dylan frowned. "What's wrong with him?" he asked. "And what's a 'tuffet'?"

"He'll do anything for an edge – shatter a shinbone with a stamp of his boot or use fake fat in his butter-crunch," Father Goose sighed. "He's a bad egg."

"Why would he steal cows?" Max asked. "To get free milk?"

Father Goose nodded. "As sure as Old King Cole was a merry old soul," he said. "And a merry old soul was he, so I've made my point. And a 'tuffet' is a kind of chair," he added after a pause.

"Chocolate-covered handbag!" Victoria announced, rejoining the group and waving her creation in the air. "Yay!"

"Ewww!" Allie gasped, goggling at her ruined handbag. "What have you done?!"

Victoria's big blue eyes filled with tears. "You

said I could dip anything. You said be creative . . ."

"OK, OK," said Allie hastily before the little girl burst out crying. "Don't cry. Just . . . don't pay so much attention to what I say."

"That's what I do," Dylan assured the little girl. "It works quite well."

Jo folded her arms and drummed her fingers on her elbows. "I guess we should pay this Wally Caldwell a little visit," she said. "He might need to spend some time in the Sin Bin."

"Um, Allie?" said Max as Allie looked sadly at her bag. "If you're not going to eat your handbag, can I have it? It looks tasty."

Chapter Five

Wally Caldwell's place was completely different to Father Goose's. An old farmhouse stood beside a barn and a fenced-in field. A bull grazed in an adjoining pen.

The Five walked up to the door and knocked firmly. They heard limping steps. The door flew open with a bang.

"Caldwell opens the door!" roared an angry-looking red-bearded man in the style of a sports commentator. "He doesn't recognize the kids and the mutt. Ohhh, you can tell he's not happy!"

Jo cleared her throat. "Erm . . . we wanted to talk to you about some cow thefts . . ."

"And can I have an autograph?" said Dylan hopefully. "Just make it out to 'Lucky Winning Bidder'."

Wally Caldwell glared at them. "I've got a business to run," he growled. "I don't have time to talk to kids." He put on his sports announcer voice again. "Oh – offside! Caldwell shows the yellow card!"

And he slammed the door in their faces.

"Let's make a note not to come Christmas

carolling at this house," said Allie after a tricky pause.

"I still want to know why his ice-lolly stick was in Cleopatra's stall," said Jo. "And why he won't talk to us."

"He told us – we're offside," Dylan pointed out.

"Well, as long as we're *off*side, let's look *in*side," Jo said, tossing her dark brown hair in determination. She pointed. "Maybe Cleopatra's in his barn."

Jo, Dylan Max and Timmy headed for the barn. Victoria picked up a nearby garden hose and swung it. "I'm thirsty," she said. "Can I have a drink?"

"I guess," Allie said absently, staring after the others. "Just don't get creative."

Victoria picked up the hose, turned it on and squirted Allie.

"Hey!" Allie spluttered in shock.

"It's not me – the *hose* is creative," said Victoria brightly. "It thinks it's a snake!"

Allie did her best to evade the water, but couldn't get out of range. Victoria finally turned it off. "Bad hose," she scolded. "It's sorry," she told Allie. "I'm making it sit quietly by itself." She dropped the hose and scampered around the corner of the house as Max, Jo, Dylan and Timmy came back from investigating the barn. They gawped at the bedraggled Allie.

"Constable Stubblefield doesn't need me to babysit," Allie said through gritted teeth. "She's got a perfectly good jail cell Victoria could be locked up in."

Max fanned the air. "The barn had plenty of cows and plenty of flies and plenty of stink, but no Cleopatra," he told Allie.

A scream ripped through the air. The Five hurtled round the corner, to see Victoria standing in the middle of the bull's paddock, staring at the enormous creature with terror. The bull didn't look very pleased to see her. It was pawing the ground and snorting.

"OK, Victoria, stay very quiet," said Allie in an ultra-calm voice. "Don't make a—"

Victoria screamed at the top of her voice. The bull bellowed and began to charge.

Max and Dylan grabbed the tarpaulin draped over a nearby woodpile. They rushed across, waving it. "*Olé!*" they roared, dancing out of the way as the bull charged them and crashed into a big stack of hay bales.

Allie raced into the paddock and seized Victoria. Shaking its head groggily, the bull gave chase. Timmy ran out and barked until the bull decided to chase *him* instead.

Timmy ran as fast as he could, but the bull was gaining on him.

Jo screeched up on her bike, towing a small cart containing a scarecrow. In the scarecrow's twiggy hands was a checked tablecloth, which flapped like a matador's cape. The bull stopped chasing Timmy, looking confused. It pawed the ground and snorted. Then it turned towards the scarecrow.

Jo unhitched the cart from the back of her bike as quickly as she could, then jumped the bike over the field fence to safety.

The bull thundered down on the scarecrow and butted it, sending it flying through the air. It landed on Allie, who wrestled it to the ground.

"Allie's dancing with a scarecrow!" Victoria squealed with delight, her fear forgotten. "Allie's in love with a scarecrow! Why don't you marry him?"

"How come bulls are so angry all the time?" Max

panted, pushing his fringe out of his eyes as the Five gathered together again. "They should take a holiday and chill out. Aruba – that's supposed to be very nice."

Jo crossed to the bull's pen. Its gate was open, leading straight into the field. "This gate was closed when we got here," she said. "Somebody let him out on purpose!"

Chapter Six

Dylan spotted something on the ground. He pounced. "And I think I know who did it," he said, standing up and waving a familiar looking ice-lolly stick in the air. "Caldwell wanted to scare us away."

"What's his problem?" Jo said crossly. "What's he hiding?" She glanced back at the garage. Her eyes widened. "And more importantly," she added, "where's he going right now?"

The garage door swung open. A four-wheel-drive roared out, Wally Caldwell at the wheel.

"Caldwell's wide open!" bellowed Wally Caldwell in his sports announcer voice. "No one can catch him now!" And he added some cheering sound-effects as the four-by-four roared off into the distance, leaving a dusty trail behind.

Jo tutted. "I'm getting irritated with this Caldwell bloke," she said, grabbing her bike and hopping on.

The others copied Jo, grabbing their bikes and streaking after Caldwell. The ex-rugby player had left a trail of destruction that was easy to follow: broken bushes, smashed fences, snapped saplings. Victoria clung on to the back of Allie's bike, alternately pulling Allie's hair and covering her eyes as the Five tore after their target. Allie was struggling to keep her bike upright.

The off-road trail ended at a tarmac road.

"Where'd he go, Timmy?!" Jo panted, snapping her head left and right.

Timmy sniffed out Wally Caldwell's scent, leading them up the road to a field full of pumpkins. A tell-tale trail of pulped fruit showed the Five exactly which way Wally Caldwell and his four-by-four had gone.

Allie struggled on, peering through Victoria's grabbing fingers. Pieces of mashed-up pumpkin flew at her, dolloping onto her clothes. Victoria let go of Allie's hair for a moment and held out her arms, pretending to be an aeroplane. The bike got even harder to steer.

"Fly, Allie, fly!" Victoria commanded, giggling madly.

"Flying probably isn't gonna happen," Allie panted. "*Crashing* I'm pretty confident about."

Timmy led them on through a wheat field, following a trail where the crop had been beaten down. They crashed out of the far side – and found themselves at Constantine Tarlev's crazy golf course.

Wally Caldwell's four-by-four was parked near the course's mascot: a six-metre-high fibreglass statue of a grinning Constantine, holding an enormous golf club.

"Constantine Crazy Golf!" the mascot bellowed in a booming, electric voice. "Ha, ha ha – enjoy game now! Constantine Crazy Golf! Ha, ha ha – enjoy game now!"

"Ooh, crazy golf!" Victoria squealed. "I want to play!"

"Shh," said Allie, getting off her bike with difficulty. "In a minute. Be quiet."

The Five crept up to the window of Constantine's snack bar. Allie wiped squashed pumpkin off her face.

Wally Caldwell was talking to Constantine. He looked mean and threatening.

"Listen, Tarlev, I expect you to buy all your ice cream from me," Wally snarled. *"End of story."* He broke into his announcer voice. "Oooo!! Caldwell scores!"

"Constantine carries Father Goose ice cream!" Constantine said defiantly. "Constantine not scared of crazy red-beard man!"

"I *always* get what I want," Wally Caldwell said, wagging his finger in Constantine's face. "And I want you to sell my ice cream. Next time I'm not going to be so friendly!"

He limped off, throwing Constantine a scary look. Two seconds later, he was back, sheepishly picking up something lying on the counter. "Forgot my keys," he mumbled, backing out again.

From their spot behind the snack bar, the Five watched Caldwell stomping towards his four-by-four. Jo leaped out and trotted after him.

"We're not on your property now," she called. "Why can't you answer some questions?"

Caldwell pulled an air-horn from his pocket – the kind of thing sports fans set off at matches. Jo jumped out of her skin as he blasted it at her.

PPPAAAARRRPP!

Dylan tried to help Jo. "We just want to know i—"

PPPAAAARRRPP! Caldwell blasted it at Dylan as well.

"But y—"

PPPAAAARRRPP!

"Why di—"

PPPAAAARRRPP!

Caldwell got into his four-by-four and tore away, leaving a billowing dust trail. He stuck the air-horn out of the window for one last blast. Helpless, the Five watched him drive away.

"We have to watch him closely," Jo said through gritted teeth.

"OK," Dylan agreed. "But we should check some other farms tomorrow. It's been a long day."

Chapter Seven

The Five made for their bikes. Victoria stopped them.

"Allie said I could play crazy golf!" she wailed. "Shedidshedidshedidshedid . . ."

Allie threw her hands in the air. "OK, fine," she said. "One round, then we go home."

A few minutes later, the six-year-old was lining up her putter for the first hole, featuring a fairy castle.

"OK, hole number one," Allie explained. She pointed. "You hit it over the drawbridge and into the hole on the other side."

Victoria hit her golf ball. It rolled up a slope

towards the drawbridge, hit the side of the bridge and rolled back.

"I have to hit it again," she announced.

She lined up. Blam. Same thing.

"I have to hit it again," Victoria repeated.

She hit it for a third time, with the same result. Allie sighed.

The sun was starting to sink in the sky as Victoria's ball rolled back to her feet.

"I have to hit it again," said the six-year-old stubbornly.

Allie heaved an even bigger sigh as Victoria's ball rolled back once again.

It was dark when Constantine poked his head out of the snack bar door. "Constantine is closing up!" he shouted at the Five and Victoria, who was still plugging away at the fairy castle. "Looking forward to bubble bath and toy boat."

Jo had had enough. Picking up Victoria's ball, she carried it to the hole and dropped it in. "There," she said. "A hole in one. Can we go now?"

Back in the snack bar, Constantine was removing his apron. A masked figure leaped on him from behind, put a sack over his head, shoved him in the broom cupboard and slammed the door.

The masked figure grabbed the large lever on the main circuit box controlling the crazy golf course. It overloaded. Sparks flew. The golf course started going crazy.

The Five spun round and stared as lights flashed on and off.

"ConstantineCrazyGolfHaHaHaenjoygame now!" squealed the mascot as the tape loop sped up. The fairy castle drawbridge bounced up and down rapidly, walloping the moat and drenching the kids in waves of water.

"Did I do that?" Victoria gasped, gazing at the wildly bouncing drawbridge. "Cooool . . ."

Now the Jack-in-the-box sprang out of its box. To avoid its jabbing, grinning head, the Five fled to the merry-go-round. Things were no better there. The merry-go-round spun so fast that their feet left the ground. They clung on for dear life as they whizzed round.

"Woaaah!"

One by one, they leaped off the merry-go-round and landed in the bushes. Struggling back to their feet, they ran back to the snack bar. Victoria lagged behind, wailing. Allie gave her a piggyback ride, grunting: "Ohh – eeh – oww . . ." as Victoria grabbed handfuls of her hair and poked her in the eyes.

Timmy barked madly at the broom cupboard. The kids flung the door open. Constantine lay slumped in a heap, the sack still on his head. Max pulled off the sack, and the kids helped him over to the circuit board. Looking completely dazed, Constantine pressed a couple of buttons. Everything stopped.

"Are you OK, Constantine?" Jo asked anxiously.

"Constantine never realize how much his head smell before being trapped in sack with it," said Constantine, looking a bit sick. "Other than this, Constantine OK."

Dylan shook his head. "'Fraid not, Constantine," he said, as kindly as he could. He pointed at the freezer door. It was broken off its hinges. Items were scattered all over the floor. "You've been robbed again."

The Five gawped at the mess.

Constantine took one look, and pulled the sack back on.

Chapter Eight

Victoria had watched everything with interest. Now she trotted over to the cola tap. "Constantine?" she said in a sweet voice. "Can I have a little drink?"

Constantine waved a heavy, rather sad hand in the air. "Of course, little blond girl."

Delighted, Victoria turned on the cola tap and squirted it straight into her mouth.

Jo studied the contents of Constantine's cash register as Victoria made her way down the line of flavoured drinks. "They didn't take the money," she said, pushing the drawer closed. "What were they after?"

"Maybe they're sort of Zen-like thieves who reject material goods," Max suggested.

Jo raised her eyebrows. "Then what would they steal?" she asked.

Max paused, thinking. "Peace. Goodwill," he said at last. "Onion rings."

Constantine came out of the walk-in freezer after checking his stock. "Only thing missing is new shipment of Red Riding Hood Crunch ice cream," he said.

"That's a Father Goose ice cream, right?" said Dylan.

"Hey!" Jo said in excitement, "Caldwell threatened Constantine about Father Goose ice cream!"

Victoria had reached the end of the line of fizzy drink taps. "All done!" she said.

"Ah, adorable little girl drink her fill!" Constantine cooed. He totted up the bill briskly on a notepad. "Kirrins owe thirty-two pounds ten pence," he said. "Constantine not running charity."

"Hey," said Dylan, emerging from behind a stack of sweet boxes, "why didn't you tell us you had a security camera?"

Constantine opened a cupboard, revealing a monitor. "Constantine not like way camera make him look," he explained, as he rewound the tape. "Camera adds five kilos to Constantine."

Everyone gathered around to watch the film of a masked thief coming out of the freezer, carrying a case of ice cream. He had a red beard – and was walking with a limp.

"Caldwell!" Jo gasped.

Max looked closer. "No, wait," he said, holding up his hand. "Caldwell injured his *right* knee playing rugby. That guy is limping on his left leg."

The thief set down the ice cream. Then he adjusted his beard. It looked like it was slipping sideways.

"His beard is fake!" Allie gasped. Rummaging in her bag, she pulled out a plastic bag with the unidentified red fibre in it. "It's the same red as the fibre from Cleopatra's stall! It's *not* couture fabric! No wonder I didn't recognize it!"

"So someone is trying to frame Caldwell," Dylan guessed.

"And I think I know who," Jo said.

* * *

The next day, the cousins were back at Father Goose's ice-cream factory in the Tasting Room. They rummaged through the dressing-up box, flinging away costumes. Jo pounced.

"Got it!" she cried, pulling out a red beard. She produced the plastic bag containing the fibre. "I knew it," she said with satisfaction. "Perfect match!"

"Good morning, Gingerbread Men!" came the voice of Father Goose. "How are the Gingerbread Wives and all the little Ginger Snaps? Ha-ha-ha-ha-ha-ha-ha . . ."

The kids froze halfway through searching the dressing-up box. They looked through the large plate-glass window that separated the Tasting Room from the rest of the factory, and saw Father Goose strolling towards them.

"Goose alert!" Dylan hissed. "You guys go and check the barn – I'll distract him!"

Moments later, Father Goose entered the Tasting Room. Dylan, who had slipped into a peasant-style costume, waved. "Father Goose!" he said loudly. "Yo!"

To Father Goose's astonishment, Dylan broke into song.

"I'm Simple Simon, the Rhymin' Pie-man, and my beats are tight, not loose," rapped Dylan, snapping out his fingers gangsta-style. *"I'm from the streets, but I still dig sweets, so ma boy is Father Goose!"*

Over at the barn, Jo, Max, Allie, Timmy and Victoria were studying a window high up in the barn wall. Allie clambered on to Max's shoulders, and pulled Jo up after her. Balancing on Allie, Jo peeked through the window.

Several cows were grazing peacefully at heavy

nets of hay. Their flanks were all marked with the silhouette of a goose.

"No Cleopatra," Jo whispered over her shoulder at the others. "All the cows have Father Goose's brand."

Victoria was bored. She reached up and tickled Max, who started to wobble.

"Victoria, stop that this instant!" Allie shouted.

Victoria kept right on tickling. "You told me not to pay any attention to what you say," she pouted.

It was too much for Max. He collapsed in a heap of giggles, bringing Allie and Jo down with him. Jo jumped up from the ground, determined to grab Victoria and tell her off. But the little girl skipped away, giggling.

"I'm not paying attention," Victoria chanted. "I'm not paying attention! Wooahh!"

"She should've paid attention," Max remarked as Victoria skidded in a patch of muck and went flying.

"Yuk!" Victoria howled. "I'm all muddy!"

"This is a cow pasture and that's not mud," Allie smirked.

Victoria's eyes widened. She took a sniff.

"EEEURRGH!" she screeched.

"Gosh. That's too bad," Jo said, totally unsympathetically. "Really."

Chapter Nine

Victoria screamed again. Allie quickly put her hand over the little girl's mouth, and gestured toward the barn. Gingerbread Men workers were leaving, carrying a big bag of cow feed.

"I didn't grow up around here," Allie whispered as they watched, "but why would you take cow feed out of the barn?"

Max grinned. "Maybe the cows ordered take-aways."

The cousins sneaked after the workers as they made their way back inside Father Goose's factory, following them to a curtained-off area near the back. Four cows were grazing from nosebags. The last cow stopped munching and mooed affectionately at Jo.

"Cleopatra!" Jo squealed, as quietly as she could. "Hi, girl!"

Max studied the other cows as Jo hugged Cleopatra's soft brown head. "There are brands from all over Falcongate," he said. "These are stolen cows. Hot beef. Purloined sirloin."

"Fee fi fo fum," came Father Goose's voice. He wasn't sounding quite so jolly any more. "I heard the scream of a little one." He shook Dylan, whom he held by the scruff of the neck. "And if this odd person had kept singing, *I* would have screamed," he added nastily.

"You stole Cleopatra!" Jo accused.

"We checked your quarterly business report and you've been doing terribly," said Dylan, wriggling in Father Goose's hand. "You need extra milk that you can't pay for."

"*And* you framed that nice Mr Caldwell," said Max indignantly.

"Well, I suppose you think you're pretty clever," said Father Goose sarcastically. "Ha-ha-ha-ha-ha-ha-ha . . ." He frowned. "Actually, you are," he admitted. He swung round to a couple of Gingerbread Men behind him. "Get them, chaps," he ordered.

The Gingerbread Men grabbed the cousins and Victoria, and hustled them away from the cows. Then they marched them through the factory.

The Five stared at the huge, gleaming ice-cream makers, milk pumps and mixers in the operational area. Allie hugged herself and shivered. The huge doors of the factory's hangar-sized freezer were flung open, and the kids were tossed inside. Sliding halfway across the icy floor, they crashed up against a wall whose shelves were stacked with ice-cream containers. One tub fell into Max's lap.

"Well, hel-lo," said Max in delight. He tore open the lid and started eating.

Father Goose walked into the freezer. "Murray, Alastair," he snapped, making the two Gingerbread Men snap to attention. "Don't let them out of your sight."

The Gingerbread Men nodded. Father Goose stepped away and pulled out his mobile phone. The Gingerbread Men promptly took out a draughts board and started playing, with their backs to the kids.

Everyone was shivering now. Frightened, Victoria clung tightly to Allie.

"Don't worry," said Father Goose into his phone. "I can assure you the special shipment will be on time. Time, time, my favourite rhyme. Ha-ha-ha-ha-ha-ha-ha-ha – oh my."

Max took an enormous spoonful of ice cream and chomped down. He pulled a face and spat something out. A gleaming red ruby sparkled on the icy freezer floor. The kids stared at it, dumbfounded.

"Wow," Allie said, picking up the ruby and holding it up to the harsh striplights over their heads. "Four carats easily. Flawless clarity."

The others gawped at her. Allie shrugged modestly.

"I know fabrics and I know jewellery," she said. "And I also know that Jupiter's third moon is Ganymede, but that never comes up."

Jo took the jewel. "And I bet this is the 'special shipment'," she said. "He's smuggling precious stones in ice cream."

Father Goose snapped his phone shut and plucked the jewel out of Jo's hand. "In specially marked containers of Red Riding Hood Crunch, to be exact," he said, with pride in his voice. "It helps pay the bills." He held up a container of ice cream and put the ruby inside it.

"Let me guess," said Jo. "One of the containers got sent to Constantine by mistake, so you had to steal it back."

Father Goose tittered. "You kids are smarter than the pig who built his house of brick. But not smarter than old Father Goose." He crossed to a thermostat on the wall.

"Now I'm going to make a new frozen treat," he said, twiddling the dial. "*You*. Ha-ha-ha-ha-ha-ha-ha . . ."

Chapter Ten

Father Goose's evil trick was a little spoiled when nothing happened. He frowned at the thermostat on the wall. "Why isn't this thing working?" he muttered, fiddling with the dial.

"I don't want to be a frozen treat!" Victoria wailed. "I'm sorry I screamed – it's my fault he caught us."

"I see, you have to take it off 'Automatic' and hold down the 'Program' button before you can set it to 'Fatal' . . ."

As Father Goose adjusted the thermostat, Max seized the opportunity to catch the old man off his guard. He darted towards the villain and snatched the special ice-cream box containing the ruby out of Father Goose's hands. Then he threw it at the stack of ordinary ice-cream containers. Everything collapsed in a heap.

The Five ran for it.

"Get off your gingerbread behinds and catch them!" Father Goose screamed at his workers. "I'll find the container!"

"Um, I don't want to be eaten by Gingerbread Men!" Victoria shouted, adding another "I don't want" to her growing list. "I won't be a spoiled brat any more."

"Good," Jo panted, running beside her. "But we need your brat skills now. Go get those Gingerbread Men!"

"Ooh," said Victoria, pleased. "I can do that!"

She darted away from the others towards a soft-serve ice-cream machine. Redirecting the nozzle, she sprayed a stream of frozen goop at their pursuers. The Gingerbread Men started walking slower as Max, Jo and Dylan added to the fun by squirting them with different-flavoured syrups. Squelching on, the Gingerbread Men kept coming at them.

Father Goose grappled with the boxes of ice cream in the freezer. Allie raced up to the thermostat and swung it around to the dark-blue snowflake that marked Extreme Cold.

"What are you doing?!" Jo shivered, as the whole factory started icing up around them.

"Making frozen gingerbread men," Allie panted.

The Gingerbread Men were walking more and more slowly as the chocolate syrup coating them froze solid and stopped them in their tracks.

Father Goose found the container he was looking for. Tucking it under his arm, he ran out of the back door and leaped aboard a silly-looking musical ice-cream van with a giant Father Goose head on top of it and a goose tail at the back. He tried to start the engine. The Five raced towards him, with Victoria close at their heels. Timmy turned and raced the opposite way.

Father Goose was starting to look nervous. He tried the engine again, and again – until it finally started up, narrowly missing the kids. The van puttered off down the road, blasting out a happy little tune.

The factory doors burst open up ahead as Timmy

pushed them open with his nose. He herded the cows on to the road, where they blocked it completely.

"Woahhh!" shrieked Father Goose. He swerved to avoid the cows, went off the road and landed in a ditch. The big Father Goose head popped off the top of the van and landed in an industrial-sized dustbin nearby as the happy music faded to a pathetic whine, then died.

"Looks like Father Goose's goose is cooked," Jo grinned.

"I'll call the police to make sure he ends up in the cells," said Allie, pulling out her phone as everyone cheered.

Later, in the barn at Jo's house, the Five gathered around Cleopatra, who was back in her stall and munching hay happily.

"Cleo," Jo declared, "we never had you branded because we thought it might hurt. But we don't want you stolen again."

Allie held up a lipstick with a grin. "So, Passion

Fruit Pink to the rescue!" she cried. "It's smudge-proof, and it goes with your eyes!"

With a flourish, she drew a smiley face emoticon on Cleopatra's flank. The others whooped.

"An emoti-cow emoti-con!" Allie announced, getting quite teary-eyed.

The kids left the barn, chatting and laughing, Victoria hanging on to Allie's hand. They stopped in their tracks as Constable Stubblefield drove up in her squad car. She climbed out with a floaty smile on her face and an even floatier gown on the rest of her. A flower nestled in her hair.

"Constable Stubblefield is disturbing in a dress," Dylan said, shaking his head.

"Let's be honest," Max pointed out. "She's disturbing, full stop."

Constable Stubblefield spread her arms, full to the brim with romantic bliss. "Well, it was a wonderful Romance Novel Convention," she sighed. "Fantastico signed my forearm, so I hugged him tight. Broke three ribs." She shrugged a little sheepishly. "He'll be OK."

"What about Father Goose?" Max asked.

"He confessed," said the police officer.

"The cows of Falcongate are safer, thanks to you Kirrins."

She shook hands solemnly with everyone.

"Bye, Victoria," said Allie, kneeling down beside the little girl. "Be a good girl, now."

Victoria squeezed Allie into a huge bear-hug.

"She will be," Constable Stubblefield boomed. "And you can babysit her any time you want."

Allie looked a little pale. "That's OK," she said, pulling herself out of Victoria's arms. "I'll stick with hanging out with my cousins and solving impossible mysteries."

The others burst out laughing. Allie's entire front was covered with sticky chocolate.

"Solving mysteries is easier than babysitting," Jo chuckled.

"Come on, everybody," said Allie teasingly. "Group hug!"

And she pulled the others into a huge, sticky brown embrace.

Epilogue

It was dark outside the house. Dylan put the videocamera to his eye and aimed it at Max and Jo, who were standing on either side of Allie.

"Sticky Situation Number One Hundred and Two," said Dylan. "Avoiding Hypothermia."

"If your body temperature falls even a little below normal, you could get hypothermia, which is very dangerous," Jo explained.

Max continued. "If you're going out in cold weather, it's important to be prepared. Wear a jumper." He turned to Allie and pulled a jumper over her head.

"And a coat," Jo added, putting a coat on Allie

next. "And a hat. And an overcoat."

The outdoor clothes were bulking Allie out so much that she was beginning to lose her balance.

"And gloves," said Max, ignoring Allie's widening eyes. "And boots. And a poncho!"

Allie was now almost as round as she was tall.

"And finally," said Jo, "in case of severe weather, you can carry an ultra-lightweight space-blanket in your pocket."

Showing the shiny little blanket to the camera, she tucked it into Allie's pocket. It was the last straw. Allie toppled sideways, falling to the ground like a tree that's just been chopped down.

"Woahhh!" Allie squealed, as Jo and Max rolled her off-camera. "Then have your friends roll you where you want to go!"

Famous 5 On the Case

The Case of the Bogus Banknotes

Read on for the
start of the Famous 5's next
Case File . . .

Hodder Children's Books

A division of Hachette Children's Books

Chapter One

Birds twittered happily in the trees overhead as the Five hiked uphill through cool green woodland. They were carrying backpacks with supplies for lunch.

"I don't have anything *against* picnics," Dylan grumbled to the others as he pushed his glasses up his nose. "But I just don't think you should have to hike somewhere to eat."

Max shifted his backpack to a comfier position and blew his shaggy blond fringe out of his eyes. "But then you're hungrier when you get there, so you can eat more," he pointed out.

"Oooh – compelling argument," Dylan said,

completely diverted. "Objection withdrawn. Let's hike for several days, and I'll eat an entire all-you-can-eat buffet."

Jo, the most sensible of the Kirrin cousins, rolled her eyes at the boys. "It won't take several days to get to Havenglen Valley," she said. "It's right over this ridge."

Allie paused and looked around at the dappled light and shade, the scampering squirrels in the treetops and the gorgeous views through the woodland. "I have to say," she told the others, "it's – *très gelato*!"

Her French accent made two squirrels wince and race away from the path. Jo, Dylan and Max looked confused. Even Timmy lifted an eyebrow.

"Why did you just say 'very ice cream' in a mix of French and Italian?" Jo asked.

Allie looked cross. "I meant 'very pretty'!" she said. "No wonder I'm flunking French. I thought it'd be easy – I'm great at French fashion and perfume and food—"

"Then they give you the old switcheroo and make it about the French *language*," Dylan put in sympathetically. "Sneaky."

"You meant *très jolie*," Jo told Allie kindly as they moved through the trees and reached the top of the ridge. "Havenglen Valley is really pretty. It's green, it's full of butterflies, it's . . ."

Her voice tailed away as the Five stopped on the crest and stared down into the valley. The valley's edges were still green and lush. But in the centre, everything was decaying. Trees were stunted and dead, leaves lay shrivelled and brown and there was no more birdsong.

"Ohh," Jo gasped, clapping her hands to her mouth. "It's a disaster area!"

Chapter Two

The cousins scrambled down from the ridge and made their way into the heart of the dying valley. They tried to understand what they were seeing.

Dylan touched the brown leaves of a nearby bush. They crumbled to nothing. "I'm no expert," he told the others, staring at his dusty fingers, "but unless this is the rare Brown Crumbly Dustbush, something seems to be wrong."

"I don't know what's going on here," Jo said. "But we're going to find out what caused this."

Timmy nudged a shrivelled brown fern with his nose. It collapsed in a cloud of dust, making Timmy sneeze.

"*Quel fromage!*" Allie said, staring at the scene of devastation.

"You just said 'what cheese'," Jo told her as kindly as she could. "I think you meant *quel dommage* – 'what a shame'."

"How come you know French?" Max said, looking impressed. "Have you been living in Paris when we're not looking?"

"I spent a summer in French Guiana with Mum, collecting plants," Jo explained.

"Did you get many?" Max asked.

"Plants, no," Jo told her cousin, scratching herself at the memory of French Guiana. "Mosquito bites, yes."

"Speaking of Aunt George and plants, let's take her some samples," Dylan suggested, pushing up his sleeves. "Maybe she can work this out."

Following Dylan's example, the others pushed up their sleeves too. Everyone set to work, trying to gather plants. Half of what they picked turned to dust as soon as they touched it. It was hard going.

Finding the end of a vine plant, Max picked it up. He followed it, pulling it up like a long rope and coiling it over his arm as he went. He was so intent

on the vine that he didn't notice a small track. Until a jeep almost drove straight over him with a honk and a skid.

A dark-haired outdoorsy guy flung open the jeep door and hopped out.

"Sorry," said Max, looking shocked by his near-death experience. "I forgot to look both ways before following a vine on a forest path."

"Hope I didn't scare you," boomed the dark-haired stranger. He held out his hand. "Rory O'Riordan. I came up here to paint some landscapes." He waved his other arm around as if it held a paintbrush. "Paint, paint, paint," he explained, pointing at the easel, canvases and other paint supplies sticking up out the back of his Jeep.

"Hope you brought plenty of brown," Jo said.

Rory O'Riordan frowned. "Indeed," he said, glancing around. "I'd heard it was pretty here. I guess I'll drive further up the valley." He gave another cheery mime, pulling his hands up and down. "Drive, drive, drive!"

"Odd guy," Dylan told Max in a low voice. "Odd, odd, odd."

"Good luck," Allie told the stranger. "I hope it's prettier up the valley."

"Well," said Rory O'Riordan, "as van Gogh would say . . ." He paused. "Actually, I don't know what he would say – I don't speak Dutch," he confessed, and roared at his own joke. "Ha ha – I'm off! Off, off, off!"

"Bye, bye, bye," said the Kirrins automatically, looking at each other as Rory O'Riordan leaped back into his jeep, started the engine and sped away.

"He could've started by painting all these plants," Dylan said, waving around. *"Plants with Brown Crumbly Dustbush* would look much better green."

Read the adventures of George and the original Famous Five in

Five On A Treasure Island
Five Go Adventuring Again
Five Run Away Together
Five Go To Smuggler's Top
Five Go Off In A Caravan
Five On Kirrin Island Again
Five Go Off To Camp
Five Get Into Trouble
Five Fall Into Adventure
Five On A Hike Together
Five Have A Wonderful Time
Five Go Down To The Sea
Five Go To Mystery Moor
Five Have Plenty Of Fun
Five On A Secret Trail
Five Go To Billycock Hill
Five Get Into A Fix
Five On Finniston Farm
Five Go To Demon's Rocks
Five Have A Mystery To Solve
Five Are Together Again

FAMOUS 5 ON THE CASE

LOOK OUT FOR THE WHOLE SERIES!

Case Files 1 & 2: The Case of the Fudgie Fry Pirates & The Case of the Plant that Could Eat Your House

Case Files 3 & 4: The Case of the Impolite Snarly Thing & The Case of the Sticks and Their Tricks

Case Files 5 & 6: The Case of the Plot to Pull the Plug & The Case of the Thief Who Drinks from the Toilet

Case Files 7 & 8: The Case of the Hot-Air Ba-Boom! & The Case of the Stinky Smell

Case Files 9 & 10: The Case of the Defective Detective & The Case of Allie's Really Very Bad Singing

Case Files 11 & 12: The Case of the Medieval Meathead & The Case of the Messy Mucked Up Masterpiece

Case Files 13 & 14: The Case of the Guy Who Makes You Act Like a Chicken & The Case of the Felon with Frosty Fingers

Case Files 15 & 16: The Case of the Bogus Banknotes & The Case of Eight Arms and No Fingerprints

Case Files 17 & 18: The Case of the Flowers That Make Your Body All Wobbly & The Case of the Guy Who Looks Pretty Good for a 2000 Year-Old

Case Files 19 & 20: The Case of the Gobbling Goop & The Case of the Surfer Dude Who's Truly Rude

Case Files 21 & 22: The Case of the Cactus, the Coot, and the Cowboy Boot & The Case of the Seal Who Gets All Up In Your Face

Case Files 23 & 24: The Case of the Snow, the Glow, and the Oh, No! & The Case of the Fish That Flew the Coop

FAMOUS 5 ON THE CASE

THE CASE OF THE GUY WHO MAKES YOU ACT LIKE A CHICKEN

Hodder Children's Books
A division of Hachette Children's Books

Special thanks to Lucy Courtenay and Artful Doodlers

First published in Great Britain in 2008 by Hodder Children's Books

1

A Catalogue record for this book is available from the British Library

ISBN 978 0 340 97084 3

Typeset in Weiss by Avon DataSet Ltd,
Bidford on Avon, Warwickshire

Printed and bound in Great Britain by
Bookmarque Ltd, Croydon, Surrey

The paper and board used in this paperback by Hodder Children's Books are natural recyclable products made from wood grown in sustainable forests. The manufacturing processes conform to the environmental regulations of the country of origin.

Hodder Children's Books
a division of Hachette Children's Books
338 Euston Road, London NW1 3BH
An Hachette Livre UK Company
www.hachettelivre.co.uk

Chapter One

It was a bright and breezy day on the crazy golf course outside Falcongate. The four Kirrin cousins (plus Jo's dog Timmy) walked towards the first hole, known as the fairy castle, cheerfully swinging their golf clubs.

"I like crazy golf," Dylan told the others as he pushed his glasses up his nose. "But it starts to get a little repetitive after the first few thousand times."

Dylan's blond-haired cousin Max jabbed the air with his finger. "That's why I've invented – speed golf!" he said. "We *run* through the course and hit the ball as fast as we can." He demonstrated. "THWACK!"

Allie pushed back her long blond hair and pointed at her shoes. "I can't run in these heels," she complained. "They pinch. Ow!"

"So do I," said Jo cheerfully as Allie rubbed her arm. She blew her dark brown fringe out of her eyes. "Speed golf sounds fun . . . but let's make it more interesting. If I win, you lot pay for my ticket to the circus tomorrow."

"So . . ." Dylan said, working it out, "if you win, I pay for you. But if I win, you pay for . . ." His brow cleared as he realized he could get to the circus for free. "GO!" he shouted, and walloped his ball.

Allie whacked her ball too, grunting with the effort. The others grabbed their putters and thumped their golf balls as hard as they could.

DOIIINNNGG! A ball ricocheted off the fairy castle. K-DINK! K-DOINK! Two balls smacked together in the air and flew in opposite directions.

The see-saw hole was next. A ball rolled on to the bottom seat and settled there. Dylan leaped on to the top seat, turning the see-saw into a catapult and hurling the ball through the air.

Balls were still flying. D-DWANG! One knocked

off a grinning leprechaun's hat. CH-CHOING! Another sent a box of golf balls flying off a shelf near the snack bar. Dozens of balls bounced everywhere.

The kids raced on round the course. A ball crashed into a ceramic fish fountain, sending the fish spinning and soaking them. Timmy the dog threw himself down just in time to duck a whizzing ball, then arched his back up as another flew under his tummy.

Jo belted her ball so hard that it bounced off both the merry-go-round hole and the Jack-in-the-box hole. Speeding on, the ball was now heading straight towards the snack bar window.

"Constantine!" Jo yelled, waving her arms. "Duck!"

Constantine, the snack bar owner, peered out of the window. "Constantine not serve duck," he said in his heavy East European accent. "Constantine serve chicken wings." His eyes widened at the sight of the ball. "Oh . . ." he said, and keeled over as it bashed him on the forehead.

The Five rushed into the snack bar. Constantine was struggling to his feet. "Constantine is fine," he said, waving his hands. "Better that ball hit

Constantine, than hit Constantine's new amazing doughnut machine."

He patted the gleaming apparatus standing next to him. "This is state of art," he said fondly. "Will make twister doughnuts such as free world has never seen."

The cousins gazed at the machine. It gleamed so much it hurt their eyes.

"There's a man who really likes his doughnut machine," said Dylan in admiration.

"Not 'like'," Constantine corrected, kissing the doughnut machine tenderly. "Love. More than family member."

But Constantine's love was not enough. The following morning, he arrived at the snack bar to find an empty spot where the new machine had been.

"Ohh," Constantine wailed, dropping to his knees. "Doughnut machine is stolen! NO-O-O-O-O! . . ."

Chapter Two

The Falcongate Victorian-style funfair and circus was in full swing. Scattered across the field were a number of small show-tents, food stalls and carnival rides. Two traditional caravans stood parked almost end-to-end, marking the entrance.

Inside the circus, the Kirrin cousins were watching a juggler. He was tossing a banana, a pineapple, a watermelon and a bowl of cherries high into the air and, somehow, catching them again.

"I don't know why," Max said, his eyes fixed on the juggler, "but suddenly I'm hungry for fruit salad."

Moving on, the cousins walked towards a showman demonstrating a contraption that

looked like a large steam-iron.

"Behold the Morning Wonder!" bellowed the showman. "Handles all your morning tasks. As you iron your shirt . . ." he demonstrated, passing the contraption over an ironing board, while a piece of toast popped out of a slot in the top end of the iron: ". . . it toasts your bread and brews your tea!" Tossing the toast to Timmy, he opened the top of the iron and poured out some tea for Jo. "And after it's made your breakfast," he

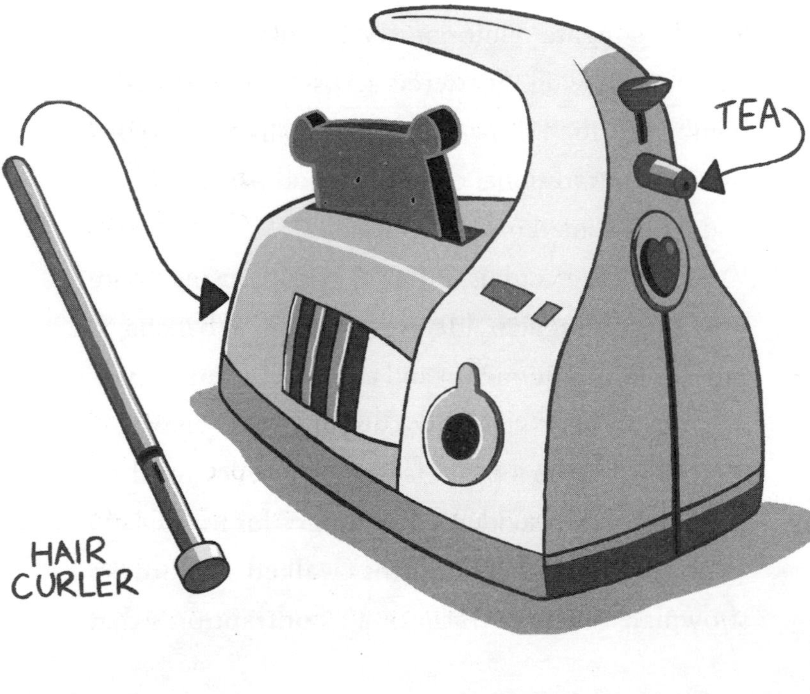

continued, "it curls your hair!" With a final flourish, he pulled a curling iron out of the bottom end of the contraption.

"I'm sold," said Allie.

"Wow," Max gasped. "If that thingamabob did your homework too, it would be the greatest thingamabob in the history of thingamabobs."

Dylan was watching the showman collect money from his customers. Respect showed all over his face. "Look at all that cash!" he said to Jo and Allie. "I've got to come up with my own gadget to sell. All right, Dylan – thinking mode!"

He scrunched up his face in concentration.

"Looks more like ate-bad-oysters mode," Allie said cheerfully.

"While Dylan's off in a money trance," said Jo as they watched Dylan wander away, "I say we go see . . ." she waggled her fingers in Allie's face, ". . . the hypnotist. Woooo . . ."

They made their way to the hypnotist's tent and pushed their way inside. The tent was packed.

Up on the stage, a man named Harry Humpston with slicked-back hair and a goatee beard was pacing the stage. His intense eyes were locked in a

gaze with Falcongate's grim twins, Blaine and Daine Dunston.

"At the sight of the Queen of Diamonds, you'll be in my-y-y-y-y command," said Harry Humpston in a monotone. "Voila!" He whipped out a playing card. Blaine and Daine snapped into a vacant-eyed trance.

"Blainc, you arc a dog," Humpston commandcd.

"Woof! Woof!" Blaine barked obediently, scratching his ear. Timmy was not impressed.

"And Daine," Harry Humpston continued, "you my dear, are a pussycat."

"Meow . . ." Daine started grooming herself, before coughing up a surprising hairball.

"And now you're locked in the same room!" Harry Humpston told them.

Blaine began barking wildly. His sister spat and clawed at him. The two of them chased each other round the stage and into the audience.

"I kind of like them this way," said Jo as the twins rolled on the ground, grappling with each other.

Constantine burst into the tent, making everyone turn round. He was out of breath and panicky. "Constantine has been robbed!" he

shouted. "Need Kirrin kids and furry dog!"

Constable Stubblefield, the officer in charge of Falcongate police station, stood up from where she had been sitting in the middle of the hypnotist's audience. "Excuse me," she demanded, "who's the constable round here?"

Constantine looked flustered. "Of course," he stammered. "Refrigerator-sized constable always welcome . . ."

Chapter Three

Within half an hour, the Kirrins, Timmy, Constable Stubblefield and Constantine were at the crazy golf snack bar. As Constable Stubblefield took notes, the Five checked the room for clues.

"Where doughnut machine was is now empty spot," said Constantine, pointing with a trembling finger at the space where the machine had once stood. "Like empty spot in Constantine's heart."

"Victim reports empty spot in heart," Constable Stubblefield murmured, making a note in her book as Constantine fell to the floor hugging himself.

Jo was studying the snack bar counter. "Constantine," she said after a moment, "the only

fingerprints here seem to be yours."

"And there's no sign of a break-in," Dylan added.

Max spread his hands. "It's the perfect crime," he said. "The criminal leaves no evidence." Spying a plate of biscuits, he grabbed one. "And I get treats," he added between mouthfuls.

"No fingerprints," Constable Stubblefield muttered, writing furiously in her notebook. "No forced entry. Just like the others."

Jo looked alert. "Others?" she said, staring at the constable. "There's others? What others?"

Constable Stubblefield leafed back through her book. "Benchley's Chemist Shop. Cash from the till," she read. "Then rare stamps stolen from the hobby shop. No clues for either."

"When did all this happen?" Allie asked.

"Saturday," the constable told them.

"The day the circus came to town?" Dylan said. "A circus full of mysterious, shady characters?"

"Exactly," said Constable Stubblefield with a shrug. "No connection, I suppose." She paused and puffed out her chest. "No," she added thoughtfully, "my finely honed instincts tell me that—"

The tinny notes of Tchaikovsky's *Romeo and Juliet*

burst from the constable's pocket, distracting her. "Oooh!" she gasped as she pulled out her phone and stared at the screen. "*One Love To Give* is on! I have it downloaded directly to my phone."

All thoughts of solving crimes disappeared from Constable Stubblefield's head as she gazed at the little romantic movie now playing on her phone screen.

"Don't worry, Constantine," said Max, patting Constantine on the shoulder. "Kirrin kids and furry dog are on the case."

Back at the circus later that afternoon, customers were queuing up at the showman's Morning Wonder stall and holding out their money.

"Excuse me mister," Jo said, striding to the front of the queue with Dylan. Where crime was concerned, Jo always liked to get to the point. "We've got a few questions concerning some robberies."

"But before that," Dylan put in, rummaging about in the large bag he was carrying, "a little item you might like to handle. I'll give you twenty per cent of the takings."

He pulled out a shoebox-sized box with a handle and a blue light on top, along with an onion, a fish and an egg. The showman's customers started to drift away. The showman didn't look very pleased.

"Behold," said Dylan, ignoring the showman's frosty stare, "an onion, a spoiled fish and a rotten egg." He dropped the food into the box and addressed the departing audience. "It's the Stink Machine!" he declared. "Get to the front of any queue! Crank the handle and gross people out! Watch everyone scatter!"

He cranked the handle. The machine's blue light flashed on and off, and a gust of cloudy air came out. There were yells of disgust as the remaining customers ran away, waving their arms in the air. One woman staggered and fainted straight into a candyfloss stall, struggling upright again with a dazed expression and a pink candyfloss wig.

"That smell! It smells like . . ." she gasped.

"Evil! Pure evil. And maybe . . . onions? . . ." answered another customer.

"I suppose it needs a little tweaking," Dylan said in disappointment, staring at the empty space where the crowd had been. He gestured at Jo. "And

now, back to the investigation. Jo."

"We're sorry, sir," Jo said to the irritated showman. "But there was a robbery last night, and we're looking into it."

"I was demoing the Morning Wonder at Constable Stubblefield's scrapbooking party last night. Made a ton of sales," huffed the showman, glaring at Dylan. "Unlike today."

"Ha!" Dylan said brightly. "Good one! So – have you noticed anyone suspicious here at the circus?"

The showman grunted. "The guy who works the Hammer ride," he said at last. "Strange guy. Leaves early a lot. Blinks too much. Try him."

Chapter Four

Inside the circus tent, Max and Allie were standing next to a handsome man in white tie and tails. The man was studying himself in a make-up mirror and adjusting his tie.

"So," Allie said, "we're just asking if anyone has seen anything."

"Not me," said the man. "I was watching rugby all last night."

He swivelled round in his make-up chair. Max and Allie gasped. The other half of him was a lovely woman with long, sweeping hair.

"And I was shopping for a new gown," she said in a breathy, girly voice.

Max and Allie looked at each other.

"It's cute," Allie said at last, as the womanly side stroked the gown she was wearing. "I hope it was half-price."

"You like rugby?" Max asked.

"No," said the womanly side at once. "I detest it."

"Keep quiet, you," said her other half, tweaking his tie again. "He's talking to me."

"Don't order me about!"

Max and Allie quietly tiptoed out of the tent as "she" hit "him" with a hairbrush while "he" tried to wrestle the brush out of "her" hands. It was too weird to watch.

Over at the Hammer – a ride where customers sat in a car at the end of a long metal arm that swung backwards and forwards – Jo and Dylan were watching from behind a barrel as the operator stopped the ride and opened the car. Two queasy-looking kids stumbled out and staggered away. The operator glanced over his shoulder, his eyes darting round furtively.

"He looks awfully nervous about something," Jo murmured.

"Maybe it's being next to half a ton of metal-fatigued machinery that was thrown together at four in the morning by secondary school drop-outs," Dylan suggested.

Jo gave her cousin a withering look. They approached the ride operator.

"Excuse me," Jo began. "Do you mind if we ask you a few questions?"

Sweat beads appeared on the ride operator's top lip. "Uh, I'm kind of busy, you know," he said in an odd French accent, pushing past Jo and Dylan to fiddle with the safety bar on the car.

"You seem kind of nervous," Dylan said. "Perhaps you're . . . GUILTY!"

Panic spread across the operator's face. He shoved Jo and Dylan into the Hammer car and shut them in with the safety bar.

"Hey!" Jo yelled as the ride started up. The car began swinging – higher and higher . . .

"No one must find out about me, I say at you!" the operator shouted, and rushed off.

As he ran, he tripped over the ride controls and knocked it into high gear. The speedometer moved close to the red marker: Danger Zone.

The car was now swinging like crazy. Jo and Dylan clung on for dear life.

"Someone get us off this thing!" Jo yelled down to the ground as it flashed to and fro past them.

"Get us off or throw us a sick-bag!" Dylan moaned, turning green.

The Hammer was a blur. The master bolt fastening the Hammer arm to its frame began to warp and crack.

Chapter Five

"Help!" Dylan shrieked as the ride hurled along. "Somebody help us!" He glimpsed something on the horizon. "Oooh," he said, distracted. "I can see our house from here . . ."

Max and Allie came running. They stared in dismay at the Hammer as it swung out of control, going faster and faster. Timmy stood at the ride's base, barking up at Jo.

"The controls are broken," said Allie, trying to switch the ride off. "And it's going into the danger zone!"

"Why does it *have* a danger zone?" Max said peevishly. "It could have a 'fun zone'. It could have

a 'yippee zone'. A danger zone is dangerous!"

Spotting a rope beside a nearby tent, Allie grabbed it and brought it to Max, who expertly tied a lasso.

"Yeehaw!" Max yelled as he twirled his lasso and caught hold of the runaway ride-car.

Timmy grabbed the other end of the rope, which had a hook tied on to it. He ran to one of the Victorian caravans marking the circus entrance and hooked the rope on to the caravan's axle. The line went taut, holding the Hammer car at its highest point.

Jo and Dylan whipped off their belts and used them to zip down the rope from the car. Halfway down, they let go and fell on to the roof of a nearby tent.

BOINGGG!

Trampolining into the air, Jo and Dylan both turned graceful somersaults and landed on their feet.

"You get a nine-point-five for the dismount," Max said admiringly as he, Allie and Timmy ran up. "Dylan stumbled a little."

Across the circus field, Jo spotted something.

"That's him!" she gasped. " That's the guy who—"

The Hammer ride operator peeked out of a portaloo. Catching the kids' eyes, he ducked back inside again.

Allie wrinkled her nose. "Was that guy gonna use the portable bathroom? Ugh, those things smell sooo gross."

The cousins ran to the portaloo and held the door firmly closed.

"You're going to stay in there till you tell us the truth!" Jo shouted.

The portaloo shook from side to side.

"I cannot hold the breath any longer," panted the operator, sounding beaten. "I confess to you I am guilty."

The Five opened the door. Gratefully, the operator slunk out into the fresh air.

"My work visa is expired," he moaned. "If I am found out, they send me back to Quebec, where my family is irritating to me."

The Five glanced at each other. Wrong villain.

"Sorry," Allie said. "We thought you were someone else."

The ride operator stood tall. "No," he

announced, "you liberate me! I can no longer live with the guilt. I shall return to Canada, with its forests and streams and delicious maple syrup."

"Could you fix the Hammer ride and give us a free go first?" Dylan asked. "If it doesn't shake your major organs loose, it's actually kind of fun."

Down at Falcongate Police Station, the Five filed into Constable Stubblefield's office. The constable was standing over a male suspect sitting with his back to the kids.

"So, you're not going to talk about all these robberies, eh?" Constable Stubblefield snarled. "Maybe this'll soften you up . . ."

She turned on a desk lamp, and shone the bright light right in the suspect's face.

"Constable Stubblefield – did you find the thief?" Allie gasped.

Constable Stubblefield swung round. "No, this is just Wax Wally," she explained. "He's a dummy I practise my technique on for when I *do* arrest someone."

The kids saw that Wax Wally was just that: a man made out of wax.

"Then he's perfect for me to demonstrate my newest gadget – Automatic Handcuffs," Dylan said, pleased. He pulled out a small, shiny box. "You see your suspect," he explained, "you press the button . . ."

He pressed a button on the box. Handcuffs flew out and latched on to Wax Wally's wrists, where they snapped tight and cut off both his hands. The hands landed on the table with a clunk.

Dylan picked up the wax hands and studied them. "And I go back to the drawing board," he muttered, before tucking the hands into Wax Wally's coat pocket.

"Constable Stubblefield," Jo explained, "we've been sniffing round the circus."

Max raised a finger. "Inside tip," he said. "Don't sniff round the Strong Man on a hot day. Phew!"

"There are people at that circus with motives for robbery," Allie said earnestly.

"The fire-eater needs money," Jo added. "He burned down his caravan with a between-meal snack."

RINGG! RINGG!

Constable Stubblefield snatched up her desk

phone. "Stubblefield . . . What? Now, slow down, slow down . . ."

As the constable took notes, the kids glanced at the spotlit Wax Wally. His face was beginning to melt.

"I'll be right over." Constable Stubblefield slammed down the phone and glanced at the Kirrins. Her face was grim. "There's been a robbery at the Dunstons'," she said.

Chapter Six

The Dunstons hated the Kirrins. The feeling was completely mutual.

"Ohh, that's too bad," Jo said insincerely.

"They were taking their 'anti-ageing/foreign language through subliminal recordings/beauty/power naps'," Constable Stubblefield explained. "When they woke up, their antique vase collection was pinched."

"That's a real shame," Jo said, even more insincerely.

"I think that rules out your circus theory," said the constable, shaking her head at the Five. "A robbery just occurred and everyone at the

circus has an alibi."

"Excuse me, Constable?" Allie said, pointing at Wally. "Your suspect is melting."

By now, Wax Wally was little more than a colourful puddle of liquid on the floor.

"You have to get to the Dunstons," Dylan told Constable Stubblefield. "We'll mop up Wally before he escapes."

Stubblefield rushed out of the office.

"I know in my bones the thief is from the circus," said Jo as Max fetched a mop. "We just need to go back there and lure him into the open." She glanced down and winced. "Oooh. Careful, Timmy – don't step in Wally . . ."

The next day, the Five approached the circus with a foolproof plan. They entered together, then split off in different directions. They all seemed to have problems with their hearing that day.

"Hey, Jo," Allie shouted. "Is it true your mom won valuable prizes on a TV game show?"

"Yes," Jo shouted back. "She won diamonds, rubies, gold and other priceless things, all of which are very easy to carry away."

A strong-man stopped bending an iron bar and stared at them with interest.

On the other side of the circus, Max and Dylan were also having trouble keeping their voices down.

"So, how's your valuable comic collection?" Max said loudly to Dylan.

"Very valuable indeed!" Dylan roared back. A contortionist unwound in order to listen more carefully as they passed. "You can see it at Fifteen Osprey Road!"

Jo and Allie were making their way back the way they had come. They pressed through a crowd of circus folk coming from the other direction.

"Hey, there's your mom now," Allie shouted, pointing dramatically. "Doesn't she have a cookie jar full of large bills and stock certificates?"

"Why, yes, she does," Jo said. She waved. "Hello, Mum!"

Jo's mum and dad, George and Ravi, appeared in the crowd. Ravi's face was hidden by a bunch of balloons.

"Oh, Jo, Allie!" said George, pleased to see them. "We just saw the most amazing hypnotist."

"He had the whole audience clucking like

chickens!" said Ravi from behind his balloons. "Your mother tried to lay an egg."

"And then I won a cactus at the bean-bag game!" George said. As a plant collector, she couldn't have chosen a better prize. She held up the cactus for Jo and Allie to admire.

POP–POP–POP–POP–POP.

The cactus needles took out all of Ravi's balloons in one go.

"Oh dear," said Ravi, looking surprised as he stared at the rubbery balloon shreds left in his fingers. "Well, we're off to see the dancing bear."

"Ta-ta, kids. Cluck, cluck!" George said cheerfully. "Oh!" she gasped, giggling, "I must still be a bit hypnotized."

"The trap's baited," Jo said, once her parents were out of sight. "We'll warn Constable Stubblefield to be on hand tonight. If the burglar strikes, she'll be hiding nearby to arrest him."

Constable Stubblefield was indeed on hand, sitting in her squad car outside George's house that night. She was also engrossed in watching the video podcast on her phone.

"Tondelaya, you're an island she-demon," murmured a voice on the screen. *"But my love for you is more powerful than the volcano god to whom you must be sacrificed . . ."*

The Five were gathered in the kitchen.

"Well, Stubblefield's in position," said Jo, peering out of the window towards the constable's car. "We'll see if the robber shows up."

"While we wait," Dylan said, "it's a great time to demonstrate my latest brainwave."

He mounted an exercise bicycle which had been set up in the kitchen. It had a blender fastened to the front, and a selection of fruit was inside the blender.

"Step right up for the miracle of today!" Dylan said grandly, getting on the bike. "Always need an excuse to work out? Love smoothies but don't have electricity? The Bike 'n' Blend is for you!"

He started pedalling. With a whirring sound, the blender started up.

"Isn't it brilliant?" Dylan yelled over the noise. "I'm going to make a *fortune*!"

He pedalled harder. In his excitement, he accidentally knocked off the top of the blender. Smoothie sprayed everywhere, covering the

cousins from head to foot.

"Instead," said Max from behind a mask of strawberry and banana, "you made a *mess*."

Dylan wiped his glasses and gazed down at where Timmy was happily licking up the gunge. "Well, that's what Timmy's for," he said.

In the living room at the back of the house, someone was quietly dropping various items from the shelves into a sack. Then – not so quietly, as a ceramic bowl smashed on the floor.

In the kitchen, the cousins froze. Timmy rushed towards the living room in a frenzy of barking. Coming to their senses, the kids ran after him. They were just in time to see a dark figure climbing out of the window, clutching a bag of loot.

Chapter Seven

The figure dropped to the ground and started to run. The kids flung themselves out of the window and followed him to a hedge on the edge of the property.

Constable Stubblefield was still engrossed in her video podcast.

"Hang on, Tondelaya! I can carry you across this molten lava, broken collarbone or no!"

The thief made it over the hedge. So did the cousins. The thief fled past the squad car with the Five in pursuit. Then he came running back again, with the Five still hot on his tail.

The figure raced on through a tomato field as Jo

hurled ripe tomatoes at his back.

One tomato caught the figure a ringing blow on the back of the head. He tripped and fell.

Constable Stubblefield had finally seen what was going on. She put her squad car in gear and roared down the tomato field.

Timmy reached the fallen thief. Growling, he stood guard while the others raced towards him. Then he sniffed the figure. His growl turned to a puzzled whine.

The kids arrived. Jo knelt down. The figure rolled over. Moonlight shone on a familiar face.

"*Mum?!*" Jo gasped.

Her siren blaring and her blue lights flashing, Constable Stubblefield pulled up her squad car. The kids squinted in the brightness.

George sat up groggily. She looked confused. "What am I doing here?" she said. "Why am I covered with tomato? Why do I have my silver cutlery in a bag?"

Constable Stubblefield hopped out of the car, twirling her baton. "All questions for the jury," she said, and slapped handcuffs on George's wrists. "You, my good madam, are nicked,"

she continued, "on a charge of burglary."

"Mum?" Jo said again.

And the Five watched in consternation as the police officer led George away.

"Why would Aunt George want to rob herself?" Max demanded down at the police station the following day. "It makes no sense. And believe me, *I* usually don't make sense, so I know what I'm talking about."

"She staged her own robbery so no one would suspect her of the others," explained Constable Stubblefield as the rest of the Five crowded round wanting an answer to the same question.

"Maybe I was sleepwalking," George said apologetically, from behind the bars of her jail cell. "I once played Tchaikovsky's Violin Concerto in my sleep. Which is strange because I don't know how to play the violin, and I prefer Mozart."

Stubblefield reached down and dumped the bag of loot on her desk. "Quite a haul for somebody napping," she said. "China, rare books, silver." She held up an ornate antique key. "Old brass key . . ."

George looked puzzled. "Where'd that come

from?" she said, staring at the key in the constable's hand. "It's not mine."

"Maybe you bought it in your sleep," said Constable Stubblefield sarcastically. "Ha, ha!"

"But isn't it odd that a strange key would be in there with all our stuff?" Jo pressed.

Constable Stubblefield put the key down on her desk. "I'll tell you what's odd," she said. "A two-headed cow – *that's* odd. The fact that people enjoy reality TV – most peculiar indeed. Pineapple on pizza – *you* explain it."

Dylan exchanged glances with the others.

"Hey, Constable," he said, turning back to the officer and pointing at the framed medal on the wall across the room, "could you tell me about your Bravery Medal again?"

Constable Stubblefield beamed proudly. "Always happy to, young Kirrin," she said, taking Dylan's arm and leading him towards the medal. "Found it at a jumble sale. Cost me thirty quid. True story."

Dylan winked over his shoulder at the others. Allie quickly swiped the key from the desk and put it in her pocket.

"Now," said Constable Stubblefield, heading

towards George's jail cell, "if you'll excuse me, I have to fingerprint your beloved Auntie . . ."

In George's study later that day, Jo, Max and Allie pored over a pile of books. Dylan was on his laptop.

Max picked up the key and studied it. He leafed through the pages of one of the books and stared hard at a picture he'd found. "Well, it's definitely not an antique Italian skeleton key," he concluded. He looked perplexed. "Why would you want to unlock an antique Italian skeleton?"

"It's not a grandfather clock key," Allie added, flipping through another book.

Dylan clicked his keyboard. "Bingo!" he shouted.

"Did you find it?" Jo said eagerly.

Dylan shook his head. "No," he said. "It's a website where you can play Bingo."

He turned his laptop so the others could see the animated Bingo game.

Jo gave him a flinty stare.

"What?" Dylan said. "I could win a jet-ski."

Jo turned back to her book with a sigh. She flipped a page.

"Wait," she said, sitting up. "I think I've got it!"

The others gathered round her. The page showed an illustration of a key which matched theirs.

"Steamer trunk key, circa Victorian era," Jo read.

"Victorian-era circus," Dylan said slowly. "Victorian-era key . . . I think we know what that means."

"The robber's over a hundred and thirty years old!" Max gasped.

"It means it's evidence that the robber is from the circus," Allie explained patiently to Max. "If we find the lock this key opens, I bet we find the robber."

Jo made a decision. "Allie, you and Max go and check it out," she said, getting to her feet. "Dylan and I are going to visit Mum first."

Chapter Eight

Max and Allie headed for the circus. As soon as they reached the entrance, Max pulled out the key. "All right," he said, weighing it in his hand. "Let's find the lock this key opens."

They moved round the circus, trying to find things to unlock. Max spotted a trunk inside one of the tents.

"OK, key," said Max optimistically, as Allie kept guard outside the tent. "Open this lock."

Nothing happened.

Next they tried their luck on the cage containing the circus's dancing bear.

"OK, key," Max tried again. "Open *this* lock."

Once again, nothing happened – which was probably just as well. The bear wasn't the friendliest animal they'd ever seen. Feeling more pessimistic, Allie and Max tried another tent and another trunk.

"OK, key," Max said. This was becoming a little repetitive. "Open *this* lock."

Nothing. Zip. *Nada*.

"Oh, you're killing me, key," Max muttered.

Allie noticed the Victorian circus caravans flanking the entrance. "Wait," she said, seizing Max's arm. "These caravans! We haven't tried them!"

They ran to the first caravan in the line. Allie put the key in the lock and took a deep breath. "OK, key," she said. "*Please* open this lock."

Allie wasn't sure who was more shocked, her or Max, when the key smoothly opened the caravan door. "See?" she said, recovering. "If you say please, good things happen."

The caravan door burst open. Max and Allie were buried in an avalanche of loot. Paintings, vases, candelabras . . . *and Constantine's doughnut machine*!

* * *

Back at the police station, Constable Stubblefield was still trying to get an answer out of George.

"So, you won't confess, eh?" she said, looking sternly through the bars of George's jail cell. "You leave me no choice about what to do now." She checked her watch. "I'm going to lunch, then I'll ask you again later."

Jo and Dylan arrived just as Constable Stubblefield had left.

"We got all the stuff you asked for, Mum," said Jo, passing items to her mother through the bars. "Your toothbrush. Botany textbook. Ventriloquist's dummy. And a pack of cards to play Patience."

"And I came up with a new gadget," Dylan said proudly. He reached into George's cell and placed a visor with two hanging robotic arms on George's head. "It's an automatic backscratcher so your hands will be free to twiddle your thumbs while you rot in captivity," he explained.

Dylan hit a switch on the visor. The arms went crazy, tickling George so much that she dropped all the goodies Jo had just handed her. Switching off the arms with some difficulty, she took the visor off, laughing: "Maybe I'll just stick with Patien—"

As if someone had flipped a switch, George went into a trance. She reached down to pick up the Queen of Diamonds from the pack of playing cards, now lying scattered on the floor.

"Mum?" Jo said.

"Must bring loot to Harry," George mumbled. She started searching round her cell.

Dylan frowned. "Wasn't the Queen of Diamonds the card the hypnotist showed to people?"

George was now pulling apart her bedclothes and ripping open her pillow. She dropped her food tray and cutlery into her pillowcase. "Bring the loot to Harry," she said in a monotone, adding her toothbrush to the loot inside her pillowcase. "To Harry . . ."

"Yes," Jo gasped. "He showed people a Queen of Diamonds, and they went under."

"He hypnotized the Dunstons," Dylan said, working it all out. "And Constantine. And they were all robbed."

"That's why there are never unknown fingerprints!" Jo cried. "He's hypnotizing people to rob themselves, and bring him their stuff!"

"Here's the loot, Harry . . ." said George, trying

to walk through the wall of her cell and bumping her head.

Jo grabbed the Queen of Diamonds. She held it up in front of her mother. "Mum, here's the Queen!" she said. "Snap out of it!" She snapped her fingers. George ignored her.

Jo turned to Dylan. "I don't know how to break the trance!" she said.

"We've got to get to the circus to warn Max and Allie," Dylan said, grabbing Jo by the arm. "They could be in danger!" He glanced at George, who was still trying to walk through the wall of the cell. "I don't think your mum's going anywhere . . ."

Chapter Nine

Max and Allie had struggled out from beneath the pile of loot, and were now rifling through it. There was so much of it. It was hard to know where to start.

"Those are some nice carnival prizes."

Max and Allie jumped. They looked round to see Harry Humpston the hypnotist staring at them.

"They're not prizes," Allie said. "All these things were stolen."

Harry Humpston looked concerned. "Even that lovely watch . . . ?" he said, reaching down to pluck a pocket watch on a chain from the pile. He started swinging it. Allie and Max's gaze followed the movement.

"At the sight of the Queen of Diamonds, you'll be in my-y-y-y-y command," Harry Humpston said in a compelling monotone. "Voila!"

He flashed a Queen of Diamonds. Max and Allie sighed, entering into a trance.

"Go to the cage of Brutus, the dancing bear," Harry Humpston ordered. "Go inside and take his food. Go now . . ."

In a zombie-like state, Allie and Max walked toward the bear's cage. Harry Humpston smiled

evilly and melted back into the crowd – just as Jo and Dylan arrived with Timmy. They were all panting.

"There they are!" Dylan gasped, holding his side as he caught his breath. "Hey, Allie! Max!"

He waved his arms. Allie and Max looked right through him, and moved closer to Brutus the bear's cage.

"They're hypnotized!" Jo gasped, realizing.

Before Jo could do anything, Allie had opened the bear's cage. Brutus growled. Before Dylan or Jo could do anything, both Allie and Max had stepped inside. Brutus growled again, more loudly this time, and stood on his hind feet. Timmy barked madly at Brutus, keeping the bear at bay.

"How do we snap them out of it?" Dylan said desperately. "Hitting your mum on the head with tomatoes seemed to do it . . . tomatoes!" he yelled out. "Bring us tomatoes!"

Jo shook her head. "No, it wasn't after the tomatoes," she said, remembering. "When Constable Stubblefield drove up and those blue lights flashed in our faces," she gasped. "The flashing lights! That's what breaks the trance!"

Dylan smiled with relief. "Well, then . . . I have just the thing . . ."

He reached into his rucksack and pulled out his Stink Machine. "Move to the front of any queue!" he said, using his salesman voice. "Escape the tentacles of a hypnotic trance!"

He cranked the handle. The Stink Machine's blue light started flashing as a gust of stinking air shot out of the box. Allie and Max blinked in the light, and looked round in confusion.

"Are we . . . in a cage with the dancing bear?" Allie said cautiously.

"We are," Max agreed. "And I don't think he wants to cha-cha."

They flung the bear's food bowl at Brutus, who caught it and ate it. Then they dashed out of the cage and slammed the door shut.

Dylan was still turning the handle of his Stink Machine. The pong was horrible.

"Phew!" Allie gagged, fanning her face. "It smelled better in the cage."

Harry Humpston was loading his stolen loot into the back of a lorry as fast as he could. The Five raced towards the truck.

"Put down the doughnut machine and step away from the vehicle!" Max bellowed.

Harry started towards the cab of the truck, but Timmy beat him to it. Jumping up into the driver's seat, the dog snarled at Harry, who fled in the opposite direction.

The kids gave chase as the hypnotist swerved off the path and into a miniature stone castle-like structure. The sign above it read: FUN HOUSE.

"Looks like we need four tickets for the Fun House!" Dylan whooped.

And they chased the villain inside.

Chapter Ten

Blinking to adjust their eyes to the low light inside the Fun House, the Five found themselves in a long passage. Painted doors lined the walls. Scary portraits of ancestral clowns gazed down at them, and the crooked hands on a nearby grandfather clock spun rapidly counter-clockwise.

Harry Humpston was some way ahead. He ran down the passage – which wasn't as long as it looked. In fact, the whole place had been painted in such a way that the hypnotist looked like a giant by the time he reached an enormous cartoon portrait of army hero Lord Kitchener. The portrait's mouth dropped open, forming a door, and the villain disappeared.

The Five chased Harry, leaping through Kitchener's mouth and arriving in a strange drawing room. All the furniture was gigantic, making them feel tiny. It was a crazy sensation, especially as they'd felt so big in the passage only moments earlier.

The floor moved beneath their feet: up and down and back and forth. A red light flashed on and off, and an evil laugh echoed through the room.

Harry jumped across the floor, wobbling as it moved under his feet. Flinging himself at a giant sofa, he shoved it towards the cousins.

"Check under the cushions," Dylan quipped. "There might be giant coins."

They climbed up and over the sofa as Harry struggled with the handle on the exit door.

"Not so fast, Harry," said Max, spotting the rug that the hypnotist was standing on.

The cousins took hold and tugged.

"Ow – wahhhhh – oophhh . . ." yelled Harry Humpston, losing his balance and sitting down in a comfy chair. The chair spun wildly in a circle, then ejected Harry like a catapult. The hypnotist

staggered across the floor as Allie pulled down an arm on a nearby hat-rack.

"Going down!" Allie said cheerfully.

A trapdoor had opened neatly beneath the hypnotist's feet.

"Woaaaaaaaahhhhhhhh!" he screamed, disappearing through the trapdoor and sliding down a chute. He arrived at the bottom in front of a distorting mirror, and goggled at the short torso and extra long head of his reflection.

Suddenly, another reflection appeared next to him. Tall, slim, shapely – it was Constable Stubblefield.

"I need a mirror like that at home," Constable Stubblefield said, distracted by her unusually attractive other self.

Realizing she was a police officer, Harry Humpston staggered to his feet, hoping to escape before Constable Stubblefield noticed. But then the Kirrins came rocketing down the chute, slamming straight into him. The hypnotist grappled with Allie and tried to stop giggling as she got him in a tickly spot.

"It's a big day for my gadgets," Dylan said,

producing his Automatic Handcuffs box and pressing the button. The cuffs sprang out and closed on Harry's wrists.

"Now *you* are under *our* power . . ." Jo grinned, as Constable Stubblefield took one last longing look at her reflection and led the hypnotist away.

Back home, in George's garden, peace reigned once more. Max and Jo were playing frisbee. Allie and George were tending the garden. As Jo threw the frisbee, Timmy leaped into the air and caught it, landing in George's vegetable patch as he came back down again.

"Careful, Timmy!" Jo called, wincing for her mother's plants.

"He can't hurt my tomatoes any more than I did," George pointed out cheerfully. "It's lucky Dylan invented that anti-hypnosis stink engine."

"Where *is* Dylan?" Allie asked.

"Working on another invention," Max said. "A Home Haircut Kit. I don't know what it's supposed to do."

They all turned to see Dylan as he came out of the house. His black hair had been replaced by a

wild Afro, which now grew all over his head – apart from the middle bit, which was bald.

"I'm sure it's not supposed to do *that*," Allie smirked.

"I'm out of the invention business," said Dylan stiffly. "Maybe I'll try property development."

"I think you should go back to the circus," Jo said.

"Why?" asked Dylan in surprise. "I don't have anything to sell."

"Yes, but with that hair, you'd make an amazing sideshow attraction," Jo pointed out.

The others screamed with laughter. Dylan patted his new hair thoughtfully. "Good idea," he said, and rushed off up the drive.

Epilogue

Jo fiddled with the switch on the videocamera. When she was satisfied, she focused it on the empty biscuit tin sitting on its side on the kitchen counter.

"Sticky Situation Number Thirty-Nine," she said into the mike. "You Have To Take Fingerprints."

Max came into shot to study the biscuit tin. Jo panned the camera across to Allie.

"Identifying fingerprints has become an exact science," Allie began.

"We've already dusted the empty biscuit tin with graphite powder, and lifted the fingerprints with tape," Max added in the background.

Dylan popped into view, holding up his

laptop. "And we've loaded the images on to my computer, to match the ridges and furrows of the fingerprints, so we can see who stole all the biscuits," he explained.

He hit a button. A paw print appeared on the screen.

"In this case," Dylan said, "the fingerprints are a paw print."

Everyone looked at Timmy. Timmy looked guilty.

"Run, Timmy, run!" Jo advised.

Timmy ran, with Max, Allie and Dylan chasing after him.

Jo put down the camera and got a fresh biscuit tin from one of the kitchen cupboards. Allie's voice yelled: "Timmy, come back!" somewhere halfway down the garden.

"It leaves more biscuits for me . . ." Jo said happily, prising off the lid and helping herself.